The Best Christmas Ever

by Sylvia Green
Illustrated by Chris Chapman

A
LITTLE APPLE
PAPERBACK

SCHOLASTIC INC.
New York Toronto London Auckland Sydney
Mexico City New Delhi Hong Kong Buenos Aires

For my parents

No part of this publication may be reproduced in whole or in part, or stored in a retrieval system, or transmitted in any form or by any means, electronic, mechanical, photocopying or otherwise, without written permission of the publisher. For information regarding permission, write to Scholastic Children's Books, Commonwealth House, 1-19 New Oxford Street, London WC1A 1NU, UK

ISBN 0-439-34013-6
Text copyright © 2000 by Sylvia Green
Illustrations copyright © 2000 by Chris Chapman

All rights reserved. Published by Scholastic Inc., 555 Broadway, New York, NY 10012, by arrangement with Scholastic Children's Books, UK. SCHOLASTIC, LITTLE APPLE PAPERBACKS, and associated logos are trademarks and/or registered trademarks of Scholastic Inc.

12   11   4   5   6/0

Printed in the U.S.A.   40
First Scholastic printing, November 2001

Chapter 1

I'm Not Staying Here!

"They might want to stay in that strange house. But I don't." With two leaps and a bound, Puss ran across the sidewalk they called a front yard.

"I'm going home — before Ginger Tom takes over my territory. All that time and effort I put into defending it . . . How dare they take me away."

The sudden noise of the traffic was deafening as Puss skidded across the sidewalk. He kept his head down and ran. Around the corner and around the next. Over a wall and through a garden.

"And as for shoving me in that basket . . ." His ears twitched at the thought of it. He was usually put in *that* basket to go to someone called the vet. Puss didn't like that, either, but at least you got to go home again after the vet had stuck needles in you.

"Which way?" He leaped onto a high wooden fence and sniffed the air for familiar smells. "Ah-choo!" The traffic fumes were getting up his nose. "How can you smell anything around here?"

His long black tail swished from side to side as he looked up and down the street. "Houses. Nothing but houses. Where are the fields? Where are the trees?"

He cringed as yet another truck thundered by. "Ye-owl!" Puss was used to a few cars coming through town, but this was dreadful — they never stopped. "Why on earth did Jenni want to come and live *here?*"

He spotted a tabby cat sitting on top of a red car that was parked in a driveway. "I'll ask him where the fields are."

Puss jumped down and walked over to the cat, his tail gently curved in a friendly way. "Excuse me." He thought he'd better be polite — after all he was a stranger here.

The tabby cat immediately stood up and arched his back. His fur bristled to the end of his tail. "Ssss-stay back! Keep your distance!" he spat. "Don't even think about trying to take over my territory."

Puss jumped back. "How rude." No cat

in his town would have dared to speak to him like that. They knew their place — they respected him. Well, Ginger Tom did annoy him sometimes — but Puss soon showed him who was boss.

"You call that a territory?" Puss gave the hissing, spitting cat his "special stare." "What would I want with a tiny patch of gravel with a car parked on it?" he growled. "And only one measly bush? You should see my territory — it's enormous. It's got loads of bushes. And trees to climb and lots of grass . . ."

The tabby cat wasn't interested. He crouched down and let out a low, warning yowl.

Puss gave an irritated flick of his tail. "It's no use asking him anything. He's obviously got no idea about the finer things in life."

With his head held high, he stalked off. Puss — the fearless cat — had never needed anybody's help before. "And I don't need it now," he said.

Around the corner there was a row of

different buildings. Puss stared up at the big windows full of gold and glitter.

"Stores." He'd only ever seen the stores in his town from the car on the way to see the vet. And he'd never taken much notice — he was too busy sulking at having been shoved in that basket again. But he knew about the stores — that was where Jenni's mom got his cat food.

He started to run. "The fields will be just up here. And then I'll be home."

He gradually slowed down as he got past the stores. There were no fields. Just more houses.

These were not the stores he knew.

He kept walking, his ears pricked for familiar sounds. "How can I hear the cows mooing or the field mice squeaking with all this traffic?"

He glanced down to check his white

front feet. His boots, Jenni called them. She often called him Puss in Boots because he was all black with four white feet. His boots were definitely looking grungy, but he couldn't stop to wash them now.

"They actually expected me to *stay* at that house," he grumbled. "They told me I had to get used to it and then I could go out in the backyard. You call that a backyard? That tiny square of grass I saw from the window? Huh! I'm going back to my own yard — my own territory."

He stopped and looked all around him. Nothing was familiar — he couldn't see anything he recognized.

Then, through the traffic, he caught a glimpse of something ginger-colored on the other side of the road. It was a cat.

"It's Ginger Tom!" cried Puss. He actually felt pleased to see him. "If he's here, then home must be just around the corner. I bet he's on his way to try to take over my territory right now. I'll show him."

He tried to get across the street to him. But the traffic just didn't stop. There was only one thing to do. He put his head down and made a dash for it.

There was a loud squeal of brakes. Horns honked. A man fell off his bike and shouted at him — Puss had never been called *that* before!

Somehow, he made it to the other side of the street. He was breathing hard and his heart was beating fast. The cat was sitting on a fence watching him.

It wasn't Ginger Tom.

Chapter 2

Where Are You, Puss?

"Puss! Puss!" Jenni's throat was getting sore from calling. "Oh, where can he be?"

"I should have checked those boxes before I opened the door," said her mother. "I know how Puss likes boxes. But the way he shot out — so fast — it was almost as though he'd planned it."

"He probably had," said Jenni. "He

hates being shut in. If only he'd waited until he was used to his new home. Now the poor little thing's got himself lost."

Jenni's mother shivered in the cold December air. "We've been searching for two hours now. I think we should go back and have something hot to drink."

"No. You go back if you want to," said Jenni. "I've got to keep looking for him."

"But you'll get lost too, on your own," said her mother. "We haven't even been in East Deeming for two whole days yet."

"I'll be okay," said Jenni. "All I have to do is look for that really tall office building and I know our house is just around the corner."

As she set off again, she looked at all the unfriendly people who just walked by without speaking to anyone. In the small town where they'd lived before, everyone knew one another and stopped to say, "Good morning" or "How are you today?"

She knew Dad felt bad about them having to leave their town — and all their friends. But he'd had to move with his job. It wasn't his fault.

"Puss. Puss," she called, for probably the five-hundredth time. She passed two girls about the same age as she was walking along chatting together.

The children here already have their own friends, she thought. *I'm dreading starting my new school after Christmas. I wish I weren't so shy.*

On the next street she spotted a tabby cat, sitting on top of a red car. It stood up for her to stroke it.

"Hello," said Jenni. "You're a nice

friendly cat. I wonder if you've seen Puss. If only you could talk."

She walked on looking into all the tiny front yards. She peered under all the

parked cars. Everything felt so strange —
so closed in. She missed the big open
fields — and all the animals.

*I don't think there are any animals living
here — aside from a cat or dog,* she said to
herself. *I loved helping Mr. Roberts round up
his cows for milking. And collecting eggs with
Anna, and feeding the chickens and geese.*
She gave a big sigh. "There's nothing to
do around here."

Just around the corner was a row of
stores. The windows were bright with
Christmas decorations. But they did nothing to cheer her up.

Jenni shivered. "Perhaps I should go
back for a hot drink. And maybe — just
maybe — I'll find Puss has come home on
his own."

*   *   *

But Puss wasn't at home.

Jenni's mother had gone back to unpacking the huge boxes of their belongings. She was anxious to get the house together before she started her new job after Christmas.

Jenni begged her to call the people who had bought their house in the country. "You do hear of cats and dogs turning up at their old homes," she said.

"I know you do, dear," said her mother. "But we've moved more than one hundred and fifty miles away. He might be a smart cat, but even Puss couldn't find his way back there."

Jenni quickly swallowed a cup of hot chocolate and opened the front door to go out again. A movement caught her eye. It was a pigeon pecking at something in the street. Jenni watched in amazement as it expertly sidestepped the cars.

"Wow! All this traffic obviously doesn't bother you," Jenni said to it. "But there can't be anything for you to eat around here."

She brought it some bread and the pigeon raced toward it. He hungrily gobbled it all up.

Jenni smiled. "At least someone is friendly around here," she said.

"We'll all make new friends eventually," said her mother. "And try not to worry too much about Puss. I bet he's trying to find his way back here right now."

Chapter 3

An Even Worse Place
Than Jenni's New House

"The sooner I get away from this dreadful place the better." Puss walked through the big shopping area and the mass of human legs. He knew these stores definitely weren't the ones in his town. These were huge. And one of them even had stairs that moved up and down all on their own!

"Ye-owl!" Puss put his ears back and scampered past the escalator.

Puss was hungry. His long black tail swished from side to side. "Not one mouse to catch. This is no place for a fearless hunter like me."

There were people everywhere. He walked along trying to dodge the hurrying boots and shoes. "Meow. Watch where you're putting your big feet. Mind my beautiful tail." But at least there weren't any cars or trucks here.

A movement in a low store window caught his eye. He stood up on his back feet to get a better look. "Wow! Puppies. And kittens. And birds."

A little brown puppy with a black nose looked up at him. Several others were asleep on top of one another. "What are you doing in there?" asked Puss. "And why are you in cages? Is this some sort of animal prison?"

The puppy obviously couldn't hear him through the glass. Puss watched a guinea pig in the next cage scurry around in the sawdust to hide behind its brother.

The door opened and a lady came out with a boy who was carefully carrying a small box. "Thanks for buying me this mouse, Mom," he said.

Puss pricked up his ears. She'd bought him a mouse! You had to pay for them here! No wonder he couldn't find any.

The boy spotted him. "Look, Mom," he said. "Do you think that cat has escaped from the pet store?"

Puss didn't want to hear any more. "I'm off. I'm not going to be taken in there.

They're not putting me in a cage — and I've got no money to pay for mice."

There were fewer people out now and it was starting to get dark. Puss turned into an alley behind the brightly lit stores. His eyes quickly adjusted to the darkness and he spotted some cardboard boxes. "I'll curl up in one for a while, keep warm, and take a nap."

But there was someone there. Inside a large box, on its side, Puss saw a young man lying covered up with an old blanket.

"What's he doing? It looks as though he's in bed. Surely he can't live here? This is an even worse place than Jenni's new house."

He watched the young man take something out of a bag and begin to eat it. Puss's sensitive nose twitched. He could smell cheese. He liked cheese.

The young man looked up and spotted him. "Hello, there. You don't have anywhere to go, either?"

He looked nice — and the cheese smelled good. Puss ventured closer.

"Are you hungry?" The young man broke off a piece and held it out. "It's only a stale old cheese sandwich. It's a bit hard, but if you're as hungry as I am you'll eat anything."

Puss cautiously took the piece in his mouth. He'd never had a sandwich before. He watched the young man carefully as he chewed on it. It tasted okay.

They finished the sandwich between them and the young man patted the blanket. "Come on. We can keep each other warm."

Puss snuggled up to him in the card-

board box. In this cold unfriendly place
at least there was someone kind — and
warm.

When he woke up the next morning, just for a minute, Puss thought he was back home curled up with Jenni. Then the young man moved him to get up and he felt the cold. He blinked at the bleak alley.

The young man folded his blanket and picked up his bag. He stroked Puss. "I'm off now. Good-bye. Thanks for the company." He walked to the end of the alley and stopped to look in some garbage cans. Then he was gone.

Two scruffy-looking cats sauntered up to the garbage cans. Puss darted back into the box and peered out at them. One had long matted black fur and a torn ear. He jumped up and knocked the lid off one of the cans. It clattered to the ground and both cats leaped in.

The scruffy calico cat, which had no

tail, jumped out with something in its mouth. It was bacon. Puss could smell it. Then the black one followed with some fish.

Puss watched in amazement as they tore at their meal. The young man had looked in the garbage cans, too, before he left. "Is this the way you eat here? And you have to pay for the mice. This place gets worse all the time."

Puss edged out a little and sniffed the air again. The bacon smelled good. His mouth watered. "But I'd never lower myself to eat out of a garbage can. It's too degrading."

The two cats suddenly spotted him. They hissed at him. "Ssss-stay back. This is ours."

This was obviously their territory. Puss retreated into his box — the fearless cat wasn't in the mood for a fight this morning. "Of course, I could beat the two of them easily — if I wanted to."

The two cats eventually left. Puss didn't even stop to think about it — he raced over and leaped into the garbage can. He found a fish head, which was quite tasty, and then half a sausage, but that tasted like soap.

Crash!

He nearly jumped out of his fur as the other garbage can crashed to the ground.

Puss cautiously peered over the top of his can.

It wasn't the two cats that came back. "It's a fox!"

He prepared to run. Then he realized the fox wasn't paying attention to him. It was eating some vegetable peelings that had spilled out of the can.

"Yuck!" said Puss. "Foxes never do have good taste." He decided to make his escape and jump down while the fox was busy eating.

But the fox glanced up at Puss and then moved over so Puss could join in. Puss was amazed. The foxes in the country hadn't been friendly at all.

They ate side by side as Puss discovered some tasty bits of cheese rind and a half-eaten hamburger. The hamburger took a lot of chewing — Puss wasn't surprised it was only half eaten.

He felt good after his meal. "Now I'm going to find my territory." Beyond the garbage cans he could see the shopping area where he had been the night before — but at the other end of the alley, in the distance . . .

"A tree," cried Puss. "I'm almost home."

He bounded off toward it, leaving the fox to finish its breakfast on its own.

Chapter 4

I Didn't Know
You Had Wildlife in the City

Jenni had missed Puss's soft damp nose being thrust into her face as usual to wake her up in the morning. Not that she'd slept — thinking about him out in the cold, lost and hungry.

She shivered in the early morning air. The stores weren't open yet in the shopping area, but several people were scurrying off to work. A movement in an alley caught her eye.

"A fox," she breathed. She stood and watched it eating from an overturned garbage can. "It's beautiful."

The fox had spotted her and was watching her carefully, but it kept on eating. Jenni was amazed to be so close to a wild creature. The foxes in the country hardly ever came near the houses and were very shy of humans.

Jenni took a poster out of her bag. She'd made it yesterday evening on the computer and run off twenty-five copies. Even though people weren't friendly here, she hoped they'd read them and contact her if they spotted Puss.

She'd titled the poster PUSS IN BOOTS in big black letters to give an immediate description of the little black cat with four white feet.

A woman stopped to look at it. "Are you in it, too?" she asked.

She took Jenni by surprise. "Excuse me?"

"The play — *Puss in Boots*. I haven't seen you at rehearsals."

"Um — no. I'm not," said Jenni.

"I didn't think I'd seen you," said the woman. "I guess you're just helping out with the posters."

She didn't wait for a reply and hurried off.

"I don't believe it," cried Jenni. "Someone's putting on the play *Puss in Boots*. People will just think my posters are an advertisement for the play." She looked at the poster. Why did they have to be doing *Puss in Boots*? Why couldn't it have been *Cinderella* or *Aladdin*?

Then she had an idea. She folded over the top part with PUSS IN BOOTS on it. "It's not so eye-catching, but it still makes sense," she decided.

"Lost. Black cat with four white feet," read a voice over her shoulder. She turned to see a woman looking at the poster. "Is that your cat?"

"Yes," said Jenni.

"I'll keep an eye out for him," said the woman. "Have you thought of asking your neighbors to check their sheds? He could be locked in somewhere." Then she was gone. But two people had actually spoken to her!

"I'll ask Dad to come with me this evening to knock on all the neighbors' doors," Jenni decided.

She went back and fixed the posters she had already put up. Then she put the rest of them up around her neighborhood. A pet shop in the shopping area put the last one in their window for her.

On the way home for lunch, she spotted a neighbor just coming out of her house carrying a pile of Christmas presents.

Jenni didn't even stop to think about

being shy. "Excuse me," she said. "I've lost my black-and-white cat, and I was wondering if you could look in your yard and in your shed — if you've got one."

"Of course I will," said the woman. "My own cat got lost last year, but she turned up at the animal shelter on Sycamore Street. Have you tried there?"

"No," said Jenni. "I didn't know about it. Thank you."

The animal shelter was housed in a large, old, dingy building, but inside it looked surprisingly bright and cheerful.

Jenni stood silently with her fingers crossed on both hands as the receptionist checked their records.

She finally looked up. "No. I'm sorry, your cat hasn't been brought in here." She smiled at Jenni's sad face. "I'll make a note

of his description — and your name and telephone number. Then if he is brought in, I'll give you a call."

"Thank you," said Jenni. A box on the counter suddenly started rustling.

To Jenni's amazement the receptionist reached in and lifted out a small hedge-hog. "The warmth has woken him up."

"Shouldn't he be hibernating?" Jenni asked.

"He was," said the receptionist. "Under a bonfire. A boy spotted him and rescued him just before his father lit it. But this little guy's actually too small to survive through the winter. They need to be quite big to be able to survive a whole winter's hibernation. So we'll keep him warm and feed him."

Jenni stroked the tiny head. "You don't just take cats and dogs then?"

"No. We've got a wildlife wing. We've got rabbits, badgers, all sorts of birds, including owls, and several foxes."

"I saw a fox this morning," said Jenni. "I didn't know you had wildlife in the city."

"Oh, yes, you just have to look a bit harder for it," said the receptionist.

Jenni had an idea. "I was wondering — after I've found my cat — do you need any helpers here? I love working with animals."

"I'm afraid you're too young," said the receptionist. "But, don't look so disappointed — in a couple of years we'll be glad to have your help." She handed Jenni a piece of paper. "This is a list of things we always need here — things like newspapers and old towels for the animals' cages and runs. Perhaps you could get your mother to save some for us."

"Oh, yes," said Jenni. "And I'll bring them in."

"And don't give up hope for your cat," she told Jenni. "It's still early."

"I won't," said Jenni. "I'm going to keep searching for him until I find him — no matter how long it takes."

Chapter 5

Puss Makes a Friend

Puss left the railroad embankment — and the tree that he'd seen from the alley. "That's definitely not my territory."

He put his ears back and scampered off, as yet another train thundered past behind him. "What a racket!" He was amazed the noise hadn't bothered the badger he'd just met. It actually lived right there, by the railroad tracks.

A few streets further on, Puss spotted more trees in the distance. He instantly cheered up. "That's it. That's bound to be my territory."

The dingy street opened out to a grassy area — but it wasn't what Puss was expecting — it was wasteland. There were a couple of trees, and plenty of grass, but there was also brick rubble lying around and the remains of a building.

"Rabbits!" Puss watched them scampering around and eating the grass. He liked rabbits. Back at home there was a white one called Arabella living next door. He loved to sleep on top of her hutch.

Suddenly all the rabbits disappeared down their holes.

A loud barking from behind told Puss why. He turned around to see a large black dog racing toward him.

"Ye-owl!" He wasn't keen on dogs at the best of times. And this one was enormous. Puss — the fearless cat — pulled himself up on fully stretched legs and arched his back to make himself look bigger. He hissed and spat as he gave the dog his "special stare." Then he lashed out with his paw as an extra warning to leave him alone.

The dog hesitated. But then it lunged forward with its huge red mouth wide open. There was only one thing to do in this situation. The not-quite-so-fearless cat now turned around and fled into the ruined building. But the dog followed.

Puss ran out again. The dog followed.

Puss raced around the bricks. The dog followed.

He couldn't outrun this dog. He spotted a small gap in a wall. His sharp senses immediately told him he could get in but the dog couldn't. He dove through it, but a sharp piece of brick tore his fur. "Ouch!"

There was a thud as the dog crashed into the wall. "Crazy dog," said Puss. "Trying to get through that hole. A cat wouldn't make that mistake."

"Butch! What are you doing?" A man's voice came from outside.

Through the hole in the wall Puss gleefully watched the dog stagger toward its master. It was obviously dizzy from the bump on its head.

The man spotted Puss and gave a laugh. "Well, Butch, I see you've met your match this time. Perhaps this will teach you not to chase cats." He quickly inspected the dog to make sure he wasn't injured, then he put his leash on and tied him up to a dead tree stump.

Butch made an instant recovery and started barking.

The man bent down to Puss. "Come on out, Puss," he coaxed. "Let's see if you're all right."

"He called me Puss. I don't know him, but he seems to know me — perhaps he'll take me back to my territory." Puss ventured out of the hole.

He even allowed the man to pick him up. "That's good," said the man as he looked at him. "Apart from some missing fur, you're not injured." He brushed the brick dust off him. "There you are, that's better."

Puss stared down at the dog from the safety of the man's arms. It was barking furiously now — obviously jealous. He rubbed his head under the man's chin and grinned to himself as his actions made the dog bark even more.

"You're a lovely puss, aren't you?" said the man, stroking him. "But where have you come from? I've never seen you around here. I know all the cats." He looked down as Butch gave a frustrated whine. "So does Butch."

Puss was disappointed. He didn't know him after all.

"Are you lost?" the man asked him. "I can't take you home with me, because of Butch. But I could take you to the animal shelter. At least you'd be warm and fed there."

Puss had heard enough. "He's not lock-

45

ing me up anywhere." He leaped out of the man's arms and raced across the grass. "If I'm put away somewhere, I'll never find Jenni," he panted. What was he thinking about? "I'm looking for my old territory," he corrected himself. "I'm not going back to that dreadful house, even if Jenni is there."

Puss found himself on the canal's bank. He spotted a bridge and raced across it. Butch and the man — thank goodness — didn't follow him.

He was in a big yard. A crane was loading planks of wood onto a barge on the canal. Puss scampered around the back of some piles of wood.

A movement caught his eye. His senses were alert immediately. It was a mouse! A free mouse. He hadn't caught a mouse in ages.

Puss automatically sprang into action, crouching low and silently, stealthily moving forward. He'd lost none of his skill. A quick, excited wiggle of his bottom and he pounced!

The mouse didn't stand a chance against the fearless hunter.

A white cat suddenly appeared around a pile of wood and Puss was quick to safeguard his catch. He arched his back, his fur standing on end, and hissed at the intruder. "Ssss-stay away. Keep back. This is my catch."

The cat was holding a piece of bread in her mouth and she dropped it in front of him. "I don't want your mouse. I've caught three already this morning."

Puss relaxed a bit. "Three?"

The mouse took advantage as Puss loosened his grip. It made a break for freedom and scampered off into a woodpile. The first mouse he'd caught in ages — and this silly cat had made him lose it.

"There are hundreds more around here," said the white cat. "I'll catch one for you if you like."

"No." The fearless hunter certainly didn't need another cat to catch a mouse for him. "I can easily catch one myself — that one was a little small anyway. Did you say there were . . . hundreds . . . around here?"

The cat nodded. "And the men often give me scraps of food. She pushed the piece of bread toward him with her paw. "Jim just gave me this — he always shares his lunch with me. Would you like it?"

Puss's nose twitched. It was a piece of cheese sandwich. He chewed on it hungrily. He was getting to like cheese sandwiches.

The white cat purred and rubbed herself against him. "Why don't you stay here with me? We could have some fun together."

Chapter 6

It's Puss's Fur!

First thing the next morning, Jenni went out to buy a street map of East Deeming. She wanted to have some order in her search to make sure she didn't miss anywhere.

The pigeon was waiting for her when she got back. And it had brought two of its friends with it.

Her mother laughed. "It didn't take you long to find something to feed."

Most of the neighbors had been friendly when Jenni and her father had knocked on their doors last night. They'd agreed to search their yards and sheds for Puss. Only one old man was grumpy. He told them he hated cats because they dug up his garden.

Mrs. Armstrong, a neighbor, told her that her own cat had been hit by a car last month. But it had managed to get home and she had found it hidden in a pile of leaves in the yard. "They often hide if they're injured," she told Jenni.

Jenni couldn't bear to think of Puss being hurt. But he wasn't used to these dangerous streets. She had to find him soon!

Jenni studied the map for places Puss might have gone. "There's somewhere I should try." It was an alley behind the houses on the next street.

"Puss. Puss." Jenni walked along the alley, stopping nervously to examine every pile of dead leaves. She looked into the yards on either side.

A lady putting food out for the birds looked up as she heard Jenni call Puss. "You must be the little girl who's lost her cat — I saw your poster. He's all black with four white feet, isn't he?"

Jenni nodded. "I call him Puss in Boots."

"What a coincidence," the lady chuckled. "That's the play they're putting on over in Manningford this year. Have you seen the advertisements for it?"

"Yes," said Jenni. "Mom said that perhaps my Puss has gone to seek my fortune —

like the one in the play did for his master. But she was just trying to cheer me up."

"I'm sure he'll turn up soon." The lady asked Jenni her name and introduced herself as Mrs. Baxter.

Jenni liked her. "Do you get many birds here? I've only seen pigeons so far and a couple of starlings."

"Oh, yes," said Mrs. Baxter. "A lot come into the city in winter. It's warmer, you see — all the buildings give them shelter."

"And people like you feed them," said Jenni.

"Yes, I put out wild bird food and scraps of cheese and bread. That's for birds like sparrows, starlings, blackbirds, and robins," said Mrs. Baxter. "Peanuts and bacon rind attract greenfinches. Oh, and squirrels."

"Do you get squirrels in the garden?"

"A couple of them. Pesky little things.

But they're hungry, too, so I don't mind them having some of the peanuts."

"I like squirrels," said Jenni. "And birds. I like all animals really."

A little girl with long blonde hair popped her head over the fence. "I like animals, too. Do you want to see my rabbit?"

Jenni went into her yard. The girl's name was Alice and she was a couple of years younger than Jenni. Jenni admired Alice's fluffy black-and-white rabbit. She told her how she'd just moved from the country with her family and that Puss was missing.

"I saw something in a pile of leaves just now," said Alice. "Over there. It was moving so I was afraid to look."

Jenni's heart raced as she bent over the pile. It was moving, slowly, almost as if the heap was breathing. Her hands shook as she parted the leaves.

"Ouch!" She pulled her hands away quickly. Something had pricked her. "It's not Puss," she told Alice. "But I think I know what it is." She carefully scraped more leaves away to reveal a large hedge-hog curled tightly in a ball.

"Wow!" Alice clapped her hands. "Is he all right?"

"Yes, he's fine. He's hibernating," Jenni explained as she covered him up again. "He's nice and big so he'll be all right to sleep through the winter."

Alice looked impressed. "I suppose you know that because you used to live in the country."

Jenni smiled. "No, actually I learned that yesterday. Here, in the city."

"Will you come and see me again?" Alice asked.

Jenni smiled. "Of course I will."

After lunch Jenni decided to search by the canal. It wasn't far according to the map and it was the only bit of open space nearby. Puss was used to open spaces.

Her mother came with her. "It might be nice by the canal," she said.

"I doubt it," said Jenni. "This is a canal —

in a city. Not a nice river like we had in the country. It's probably filthy and full of garbage."

She was in for a surprise though. The

water was clean and clear and there were ducks, geese, and swans swimming in it.

Jenni smiled. "I'll bring some bread the next time we come."

They watched a long colorful boat going past and a barge being loaded up outside a wood yard on the opposite bank. The path on their side was edged with grass and bushes. A small group of people were cutting back some overgrown trees.

They went to ask them if they'd seen Puss.

"No, sorry," said a young man. "We've only just gotten here. We'll keep a look out though."

There were a girl and a boy who looked a little older than Jenni and they smiled at her. She smiled shyly back. "What are you doing?"

"We're members of CWAG," said the boy.

"That stands for Canal and Wasteland Action Group," added the girl. "Lots more of us come on the weekends. The group has cleared the canal of garbage and made it usable again."

"But it's taken a long time," said a lady. "Several years. And we're always looking for more volunteers. There's loads more to do."

Jenni's mom looked interested. "What a wonderful idea. We'd love to help, wouldn't we, Jenni?"

The girl smiled at Jenni. "Yes, why don't you join us?"

Jenni smiled back. "I'd love to. But I've got to find my cat first."

The young man gave them a pamphlet about the group. Then he suggested they try searching on the adjoining wasteland.

Jenni went there right away. She ran near the bricks and rubble. "Puss. Puss. Are you here?"

She was amazed to see three wild rabbits scampering around the remains of a building. She ran after them, but they had disappeared.

Then she caught sight of something in a hole in the wall.

"It's black fur," she cried, pouncing on it. "Here, caught on this brick. It's Puss's fur."

"Don't get your hopes up too much," warned her mother. "It could be from anything."

"It *is* Puss's fur," cried Jenni. "I know it is. He's here. Or at least he was here. He can't be far away."

Chapter 7

Spaghetti Bolognese

Puss had been walking for two days. He didn't know where he was. He could have been walking in circles for all he knew. And he was starving!

I should have stayed with that friendly white cat, he grumbled to himself. *There was plenty of food — and it was nice there.* He put his ears back as he set off again. *But it wasn't home. And I'll never find my territory if I don't keep looking. Fearless cats don't give up that easily.*

He'd found a few scraps in a garbage dump, which he'd shared with a family of foxes and about two hundred screaming seagulls. But that had been yesterday morning.

Then he smelled it. A really delicious meaty smell. His mouth began to water. The smell was coming from the back of a restaurant. "Perhaps there's a nice lady there like the one who used to give me scraps of food back at home."

The smell got stronger as he made his way down the side driveway to the back. There was a delivery van parked there and a lot of shouting coming from the restaurant. Puss cautiously looked to see what was happening.

A man in a tall white hat was doing the

shouting. "I've been waiting for this spaghetti for more than an hour." He was very red in the face. "I'm a famous chef, you know. The customers love my delicious, out-of-this-world, homemade Spaghetti Bolognese."

"I'm sorry," said the other man. "I couldn't find your restaurant."

The chef followed him out to the van. "All the meat is cooked and waiting. But I cannot make Spaghetti Bolognese without spaghetti."

Puss tilted his head to one side. He could see the cooked meat on a counter just inside the door. He sniffed the air and breathed in the delicious smell. The kitchen was empty. "Surely he won't miss a little bit of it."

The chef was still shouting at the man as they looked in the back of the van. "Now's my chance." As quick as a flash, Puss was inside the kitchen and onto the counter. He gulped down two mouthfuls of the warm Bolognese sauce. The chef was right — it was delicious.

A scream made him drop his next mouthful. The chef's face, in the doorway, had turned almost purple now. He was spluttering and spitting as though he couldn't get his words out.

Puss leaped down and cowered in a corner as the chef threw a ladle at him. "You're a monster! You flea-ridden, filthy vermin. How can I give that to people now?"

Puss shrank back as a saucepan lid came toward him. He didn't see why he couldn't give the meat to people. It had tasted all right to him — and he'd only eaten a little bit.

The chef moved toward him with a huge saucepan in his hand. Puss had seen enough. He shot through the chef's legs

and skidded out of the door. The saucepan clattered down behind him as he raced around the side of the restaurant.

"I'll get you for this," screamed the chef after him. "I'll search for you till I find you. I'll make you sorry."

Puss didn't stop running for a long time. Then he sat down to catch his breath and to have a good wash. "What a fuss," he said as he licked his right foot and rubbed it over his right ear. "I only had two mouthfuls. There was plenty left." He carefully licked all along the black fur on his back. "How dare he call me vermin. And especially flea-ridden and filthy. I've got a beautiful coat — Jenni says so."

He felt a twinge of sadness as he thought of leaving Jenni behind. She'd probably miss him. And she'd miss the mice he used to bring in for her. The look on her face when she saw him made all his efforts worthwhile. She had such fun chasing them all over the house.

He quickly shook himself. He had to move on. He finished cleaning each of his white boots and set off again.

He walked and walked. He crossed another canal — or was it the same canal but a different bridge? This place was so confusing. One time he thought he recognized a very tall building, but then he wasn't sure.

"I can't be losing my touch. Does hunger make you confused?"

Puss spent the night in an alley behind some houses. He curled up in a pile of leaves under a bush. At least it was away from the traffic.

A small terrier dog woke him up in the morning. She yapped at him through her gate. "Come and play. Come and play," she called. "I've got a ball. I've got a ball."

She looked friendly enough — even though she was a dog — but Puss couldn't stop to play. He had to get on with finding his territory. "I bet Ginger Tom is having a good laugh about taking it over."

He jumped up onto the wall of the next yard to see if he could spot anything familiar — or even something to eat. "What's that?" It was a rabbit in a cage. But Puss saw immediately it wasn't Ara-

bella. This one was black and white and a little girl with long blonde hair was talking to it.

He ran along the wall to the next yard and lots of birds flew off. Jenni didn't allow him to chase birds.

"Why do I keep thinking about Jenni?"

Puss sniffed the air. "Bacon. And cheese." He looked over to a bird feeder. Jenni often put bits of food out for the birds. He'd never cared about it before — never lowered himself to eat the birds' scraps. "But I've never been this hungry — and there might even be a cheese sandwich."

He jumped down and started to make his way across the grass. Then the back door opened and a lady came out. She gave a gasp as she spotted him. "Well, my-oh-my. Fancy seeing you here."

Puss hesitated. He was sure he didn't know her.

"Come on," she coaxed. "Come here, boy."

Puss took a step toward her. She looked nice and there was a smell of cooked food coming from the house.

"Good boy," she said. "Come on. There's someone looking for you. She's been searching everywhere."

"Ye-owl!" Puss stopped immediately. The mad chef had people out looking for him. He turned around and ran. Out of the garden. Down the alley. Down the next street, over a fence, and out onto the road.

There was a deafening squeal of brakes as a car skidded toward him.

Chapter 8

Poor Little Cat

Jenni studied the map. Puss hadn't been at the wasteland or along the canal — or anywhere else in the surrounding area. She'd been back again and again.

There was a knock at the front door and she heard her father go to answer it. It was Sunday and he'd promised to spend the morning helping her search.

"Perhaps it's someone with news of Puss." They were getting to know quite a few of the neighbors now. They often asked about Puss and even stopped by to chat. Mom said it sometimes took an animal to get people talking.

"Jenni."

Jenni looked up to see Mrs. Baxter, who had been feeding the birds yesterday. She was out of breath and looked excited. "I've seen him — Puss in Boots. All black with four white feet. In my yard — ten minutes ago."

Jenni jumped up. "Oh, thank goodness. Where is he? Did you catch him?"

"I'm sorry, but he ran away from me."

Jenni jumped up and grabbed her coat. "Was he all right?"

"He looked fine," said Mrs. Baxter. "Come on, I'll help you find him."

Jenni's father joined them and they raced to Mrs. Baxter's yard.

They searched up and down the alley and in all the yards. Alice and her mother came out to help and so did a lady with a small terrier dog. They looked around all the surrounding streets — but there was no sign of him.

Jenni didn't want to go back for dinner, but her father insisted. She was upset and frustrated. "He couldn't have gotten too far. Oh, why did he run off again?"

After dinner Jenni's mom and dad were going to the canal to join the members of CWAG. "Your father's already called to say we'll be there," Mom said. "So we've got to go. And at least you know Puss is okay now. He can't be far away. Why don't you come with us? You've been searching nonstop for five days."

"No," said Jenni. "I've got to keep looking for him."

As soon as they'd left, Jenni put on her yellow-and-black sneakers. She smiled as she looked at the tiger's face on the shoe. Puss had been so funny the first time he'd seen them, pouncing on them, then jumping back and pouncing again. She was going to thoroughly search the whole area again — he was somewhere nearby. He couldn't have gone far — she was bound to find him this afternoon.

Then the phone rang. "I've just seen a black-and-white cat," said the voice on the other end. "It was hit by a car on Market Street, I'm afraid. I think it might be dead."

"Oh, no!" Jenni uttered a garbled "Thank you" and put the phone down. She grabbed her coat and flew out of the door. She knew the area so well now she knew exactly where Market Street was.

It was only two streets away, but it seemed like miles as she raced there. She felt sick with worry and guilt. "I shouldn't have gone home for dinner. I should have stayed out looking — I bet he was hit while I was actually eating."

She turned the corner onto Market Street. "Oh, please, please let him be all right."

Her eyes immediately focused on a small black-and-white body lying in the gutter. "Oh, no!" She raced toward it. He was so still — he looked . . . She couldn't bring herself to even think the word.

She dropped down on her hands and knees. She was shaking badly as her eyes rapidly took in the black-and-white fur.

It wasn't Puss.

"Oh, thank goodness." Jenni was still shaking, but an immense feeling of relief flooded over her. Puss wasn't dead. He was still missing — but he wasn't dead.

"Poor little cat," she whispered to the tiny bundle in the gutter.

She heard footsteps running toward her and stood up to see a boy about her age.

"Saskia!" he cried. He turned to Jenni, his eyes wide with pain. "That's my cat."

"Oh, I'm so sorry." Jenni felt terrible as she looked at him. She'd been so relieved it wasn't Puss — but of course it had to be someone's cat.

The boy was obviously trying hard not

to cry. "I don't know what to do. Mom and Dad are out."

Jenni felt so sorry for him. She reached out and put her arms around him to give him a hug. "What's your name?"

"Mark."

Over Mark's shoulder she blinked back the tears herself as she looked down at the poor little cat.

It twitched!

It twitched again.

"She's not dead!" she cried.

Mark appeared to be frozen to the spot so Jenni took charge. "Where's the nearest vet?" she asked, tearing off her coat.

"On the next street," said Mark. "What are you doing?"

"Help me," said Jenni, laying her coat out on the sidewalk. Together they carefully lifted Saskia onto the coat and Jenni wrapped her up in it to keep her warm.

Mark had pulled himself together and led the way as they ran to the vet's. All the way Jenni was willing the little bundle in her arms to hang on — to stay alive.

The vet's name was Dr. Williams and she immediately connected Saskia to a drip. "It's to counteract the shock," she explained as she covered the little cat up to keep her warm. "The first thing is to get her over the shock and then we can find out what injuries she has and treat them."

They had to leave her there. Dr. Williams said it was just a matter of waiting to see if she came around.

Jenni walked back with Mark to his house. He wanted to wait inside, in case the vet called. "Thanks, Jenni," he said. "Thanks a lot for your help."

Jenni gave him her phone number. "Please let me know how Saskia does. I've got to go now. My own cat's missing and I've got to keep searching for him."

"Oh, I'm sorry," said Mark. "Have you tried looking over in the garbage dump? Or the wasteland?"

"I've tried everywhere," said Jenni. "But I'm trying it all again and again. I've got this strange feeling that I just keep missing him."

Chapter 9

Missing Jenni

Puss was really fed up. He'd walked miles and miles and there was no sign of his old territory. But to his surprise he found he wasn't so bothered about that now. He was missing Jenni. Oh, how he was missing Jenni. And he didn't know how to find her again.

He stood and watched the traffic. He was learning to be more careful — a car had only just missed him the other day when he'd run into the street. And yesterday he had heard some people talking about a cat that had actually been hit by a car, somewhere on Market Street. He didn't know if it was dead or not, but apparently a boy and a girl had taken it to see the vet.

"Wait a minute." He had a sudden thought. "If the vet is nearby, maybe I can find him. Although I was always taken there in the car ... But then, I was brought here in the car, too. It seemed a bit longer getting here — but it must be the same place."

He pictured the large man in his white coat as he walked along the sidewalk. "He should be easy enough to recognize. And he's bound to remember me — he said he'd never forget me after my last visit.

Well, who could blame me for wrecking his office?"

He gave a twitch of his tail as he remembered something called a thermometer.

"One or two broken bottles and a few scratches were nothing compared to the embarrassment I suffered. The vet said it was the usual way to take an animal's temperature." Puss paused. Did he actually want to see the vet again?

"Yes," he decided, setting off. "When the vet sees me, he'll call Jenni and she'll come and get me."

Puss stopped for a rest. He'd walked along countless streets — past houses and stores, over bridges, under bridges, in and out of alleys. But there was no sign of the vet.

"It's a wonder I haven't worn my feet

out, walking on all this hard ground," he said. "I'm sure my legs are getting shorter."

He was so tired and so hungry. He was beginning to feel weak from lack of food — and he'd had a fight with a big black tomcat. And he'd lost! The fearless cat had never lost a fight in his life before.

"Of course he was exceptionally big," said Puss. "And he had obviously had an enormous dinner — so I didn't stand a chance." He sat down to lick his sore leg where the big bully had bitten him.

"I don't understand why he was so aggressive — that tiny square of grass he called *his* yard was hardly worth defending."

He stood up as a group of youngsters came toward him. Perhaps Jenni was with them. They stopped right next to him and he quickly looked up at all the faces.

She wasn't there.

"Have you seen Puss?" one of them asked.

Puss's heart jumped. They must be friends of Jenni's. They were looking for him. He immediately ran forward, his tail held straight up. "Meow. I'm here."

They didn't hear him. *The trouble is, my deep, throaty, masculine cry is a bit weak these days*, he thought.

"I think he's going to meet us there," said a boy.

"Where?" Puss panicked as the group moved off chattering excitedly. "Where's there? Where am I supposed to meet them? And will Jenni be there, too?"

He'd have to follow them. He limped after them, through a huge gate and into a sort of field with grass and trees. But cars were driving through it and there were strange creatures in the distance with huge antlers on their heads.

"Funny-looking cows," said Puss.

It seemed a long way and Puss was exhausted. Only the thought of finding Jenni again kept him going.

They eventually stopped outside a theater.

"There he is," said a girl. "There's Puss."

"At last!" Puss looked up expectantly. But the girl was pointing to a boy. A silly boy with big boots on and whiskers drawn on his face. "Come on," said the boy. "The play's going to start in an hour."

Puss didn't know what they were talking about. But he did know it wasn't him they were looking for. And Jenni wasn't there, either.

He was tired, weak, and very, very hungry. There was a cardboard box next to the theater door and he dejectedly crawled inside. Somehow, the fearless cat — the fearless hunter — just didn't feel fearless anymore.

It started to snow. Puss remembered

snow — he usually liked to play in it. But not this time.

He curled up in the box to keep warm and watched the snowflakes falling thickly outside. "I'd have been better off staying at *that* house," he murmured.

"At least I would have been warm and fed. And I'd have been with Jenni. . . ."

Chapter 10

Jenni's Treat

"It's starting to snow," Jenni's mother called to her. "We're going to have a white Christmas."

Jenni looked out of the window. She remembered Puss in the snow last year. He'd been so funny, jumping up and down in it and trying to bite it. She thought about him all the time.

The brightly decorated Christmas tree

made her think of him trying to climb it when he'd been a kitten. And of him jumping up to catch the silver and gold decorations. He'd actually knocked the tree right over one year.

Wrapping her presents for Mom and Dad reminded her how he'd loved chasing the ribbon as she tried to tie it. Jenni didn't want any presents this year — all she wanted was Puss.

"Christmas Eve," she sighed. "And still no sign of him. This is my worst Christmas ever." Jenni put her sneakers on again — they'd be good for gripping the snow. She tried hard to keep her spirits up but it was getting harder and harder as the days went by.

"You're not going out again in all that snow, are you?" asked her mother. "You've been out all morning and you've only been in for ten minutes to eat your lunch."

"I've got to keep searching," said Jenni. She opened the front door and threw some bread to about fourteen pigeons waiting on the sidewalk. A couple of sparrows had joined them today. "And I'll be going out again tomorrow — Christmas Day. I won't give up."

"I'm just a little worried about you. You're not getting any rest," said her mother. "I'll help again later, when I've finished icing the Christmas cake." The phone rang and she went to answer it.

Jenni waited. It might be about Puss. So many people were concerned about him now. Every time Jenni went out, someone stopped her to ask if there was any news. People were so much friendlier here than she'd first thought.

And the neighborhood didn't seem so bad now that she was getting used to it. She'd seen several more foxes, and a couple of squirrels searching for their winter store of nuts. She'd even seen a badger when Dad had taken her to the railroad embankment one evening.

Dad was making her a bird feeder and they were going to have a small pond. Mr. Samuels, their neighbor, had told them that ponds in the city provided essential breeding sites for frogs and toads. There were fewer in the country now because they were getting filled in. And hedgehogs were finding more food available in people's yards — more and more wildlife was adapting to living in the city.

The canal was nice and the wasteland would be nice, too, when the members of CWAG had made it into a park. But without Puss, she couldn't appreciate anything.

"Jenni. Wait a minute." Her mother called from the phone.

Jenni's heart leaped. "Is it about Puss?" Perhaps it was the animal shelter to say he was there, safe and sound. But she'd already been there this morning to drop off some newspapers and he hadn't been there then.

"No. It's Mark, for you. I've just been chatting with his mom."

Jenni rushed to the phone. "It's about Saskia."

"She's going to be okay," cried Mark. "Saskia's broken a back leg and she's got bruising on her lower back — but she's going to recover. We've just brought her home."

"Oh, I'm so happy she's all right," said Jenni.

"Well, it's mainly thanks to you. Dr. Williams said if you hadn't acted so quickly, Saskia would probably have died of shock," Mark told her. "Mom has a treat for you to say thank you. Can you come over?"

"Oh, I don't know . . ." said Jenni. She looked up at her mother.

"Mark's mom has already asked me if it's okay," said her mother. "You go. You deserve a treat. And you need a break. Dad will be home early today and then we'll both go out and look for Puss for you."

"All right," Jenni agreed. "Thank you," she said to Mark over the phone. "I would like to come and see Saskia."

Saskia was a lovely cat. Her markings were quite different from Jenni's Puss with his boots. Saskia was black with white on her face and throat and two white legs and feet. And one pink leg — that was the broken one in a cast.

Mark was the same age as Jenni and was very nice. "I'll help you search for your cat after Christmas," he told her.

His mother was nice, too. She was taking them out, but she wouldn't tell Jenni where — it was a surprise. Jenni would much rather have continued looking for Puss, but Mark and his mother were being so kind to her. She'd have to try to enjoy herself for their sake. And she was happy to have made a friend.

They were going by car, since it was quite a long way. The windshield wipers swished away the snowflakes that were falling steadily now.

"We're going through the park," said

Mark. "Have you been there? It's in Manningford — it's very nice."

"No, I haven't been out of East Deeming," said Jenni. "I've been too busy search-ing for my cat."

She looked out of the window as they drove through the park. It did look nice. There was a lake and she saw a herd of deer in the distance. At the moment it looked like a scene on a Christmas card with all the snow on the bare branches of the trees.

They drove out of the park on the other side and pulled up outside a theater.

"We're here," cried Mark. "I'm really looking forward to this."

As they walked toward the gate, Jenni looked up at the big colorful banner above the door. It read:

THREE O'CLOCK TODAY
CHRISTMAS PLAY
Puss in Boots

"Oh, no." Jenni stopped and stared at it in horror. This was to be her treat. To watch *Puss in Boots*! Tears welled up in her eyes. She couldn't sit and watch it — not with her own Puss in Boots missing.

"What's the matter?" asked Mark.

"My cat — the one that's missing. I — I didn't get a chance to tell you before — but I call him Puss in Boots."

"Oh, no," said Mark. "I'm so sorry — I didn't know."

His mother put her arm around Jenni. "Would you like me to take you home again, dear?"

Jenni nodded. Then she looked at her watch. "But it's three o'clock — the play's just starting. If you take me back now, you and Mark will miss it, too."

Chapter 11

The Best Christmas Ever

Puss shifted in his cardboard box. Something had woken him, disturbed him. People had been walking past for ages. But this was different — it was something familiar.

"The voice. It's Jenni's voice!" He uncurled himself and peered out of his box. "Meow. Jenni, I'm here."

Where was she? She couldn't have

heard him. If only his voice weren't so weak now.

He crawled stiffly out of the box. A group of people were just coming up the path but she wasn't with them.

Then his sharp hearing picked out Jenni's voice again. "I can't make you miss the play — it wouldn't be fair. Mark just said he was looking forward to it," she was saying. "I will come in. I — I guess I'll be all right."

Puss's sensitive ears immediately located the direction — Jenni was just behind these people.

He shot off down the slippery path. As he skidded toward the group, he caught a glimpse of Jenni through their legs. "She's there — down by the gate!" He frantically tried to dodge the hurrying feet, but he slipped on the snow. Then a huge boot kicked him.

"Ye-owl!" Puss was knocked off his paws. He rolled over and over down a bank until he came to a stop up against a bush.

He scrambled to his feet again and shook himself. "I've got to get to Jenni."

But the huge boots had followed him. "Are you all right?" A man picked him up and began brushing the snow off him. "I hope I didn't hurt you."

Puss couldn't wait around to be comforted. He had to get to Jenni. So he did the only thing he could — he bit the man's hand to make him let go.

Once free, he clawed his way back up the bank, gripping on the grass beneath the snow. The rest of the people had gone now and he raced down the path. He skidded to a stop at the gate.

Jenni had disappeared. "Where is she?"

Puss spun around and saw her. She was at the top of the path now — almost up to his box.

He raced back up the slippery path. "Meow. Jenni! Meow."

Puss reached the top just as Jenni disappeared into the theater.

Suddenly there was a big burst of music and people were clapping. Puss hesitated and put his ears back. "What a noise!" But he had to go in there. "I've got to get to Jenni."

"Hey!" shouted a lady as Puss squeezed through her legs.

It was a huge place — so noisy and so many people. Where was Je —?

"Ye-owl!" Puss was suddenly swung into the air as the lady grabbed him by the scruff of his neck.

Then he was outside again.

"Sorry, we don't allow cats in here," said the lady, and laughed. "At least, not real ones."

Puss yowled and wriggled and squirmed in her grip. The man with huge boots appeared in the doorway. "I think that cat's wild," he said as he went into the theater.

Puss was dropped down into the snow. He was wild and furious. He immediately tried to get back in. But the lady was too quick for him. She closed the door in his face.

He scratched and scratched at the door until his claws hurt. But no one let him in. They probably couldn't hear him anyway with all that music and clapping and shouting. "What on earth's going on in there?"

He crawled back into his box. "I'll just have to wait for Jenni to come out again. She's got to come out sometime."

Puss settled down to clean off his fur with one eye firmly fixed on the door. He was tired, hungry — and completely exhausted. His side hurt from the kick and he ached all over. But he couldn't go to sleep. "I mustn't miss Jenni coming out."

Puss fought hard to stay awake, but his eyelids kept drooping. "Why doesn't Jenni come out? What's she doing in there?" His head nodded forward.

Puss was jolted awake as laughing, chattering people streamed out of the theater. But all he could see was a flurry of boots and shoes kicking up the freshly fallen snow. He panicked. "I'll never find Jenni in all this. Why have so many people come out at the same time?"

Had he missed her already? He joined in among the mass of legs moving down the path toward the gate. He couldn't see past them and he certainly couldn't see up to any faces.

Then, ahead of him, through a small gap, he spotted something familiar. Yellow-and-black sneakers with a tiger's face on them.

"Jenni's shoes!" But she was way ahead of him — she must be almost at the gate.

"Meow. Jenni! Meow." She couldn't hear him. "I've got to get to her. If she goes without me, I might never find her again."

Puss desperately tried to push his way through the mass of legs.

"What's going on?" said a lady.

"It's a wild cat," said Huge Boots. "Watch your ankles — he bites."

Puss got past him as he stood aside. Then he managed to push past several more people. They were all moving so slowly — but at least that meant he wasn't so likely to be kicked. If only he could get through . . .

He squeezed between a boy's legs. Then, at last, he was at the gate.

But Jenni had gone. "Where is she?" Puss frantically looked around.

"Oh, no. She's in that car. She's leaving."

Somehow, Puss gathered together every last bit of strength he had left. He raced forward and jumped up onto the hood of the car just as it started to move. His claws screeched on the slippery paint as he fought to steady himself.

The lady in the driver's seat screamed. The car shuddered to a halt.

Then the doors were flung open and Jenni was there. "Puss!" she shrieked. She was laughing and crying at the same time as she picked him up. "Oh, where have you been? And look at you, you're so thin."

Puss snuggled into her. His side hurt where Jenni was squeezing him, but he didn't care. He was with Jenni again — his Jenni.

A boy was jumping up and down on the sidewalk. And the lady was saying something about getting them home.

Then they all got into the car. Puss purred and purred as he settled down on Jenni's lap. She was as soft as he remembered and she smelled so nice. She was stroking him and kissing him on his head.

"Oh, I've missed you so much," she said. "I do love you, Puss."

Puss usually got embarrassed with all that sort of thing — but today he didn't care.

"I can't believe I've found you at last," said Jenni, tickling him behind his ears — just the way he liked it. "Although it was really you who found me. But what are you doing here? It's such a long way from home. How did you get here?"

Puss pushed his head under her chin and thought to himself that it was something to do with a mad chef chasing him. And a silly boy with big boots on and whiskers drawn on his face.

"You know what?" Jenni started to laugh. "The Puss in the play went off and found riches and good fortune for his master. And in a different sort of way that's just what you did for me. Through searching for you I've met friends and neighbors — and I've realized it's not so bad here after all. And there's lots to do."

"And don't forget about Saskia," said Mark. "If you hadn't been searching for Puss, you wouldn't have found my cat and helped me with her."

"No," Jenni agreed. "This is Mark, Puss. He's my friend. You'll like his cat — her name's Saskia."

Mark grinned at Puss. "You're a fearless little cat, aren't you? Jumping up on a moving car like that."

Puss snuggled into Jenni's lap. The boy was obviously intelligent — he'd realized right away what a fearless cat he was. The woman looked okay, too. And anyway, he'd just made a decision. From now on anywhere Jenni wanted to be was okay with him.

"And there's a nice rabbit that lives just around the corner," Jenni told him. "You like rabbits, don't you? This one belongs to Alice — you'll like her, too. Then there's a friendly lady who feeds the birds . . ."

Puss closed his eyes as Jenni talked softly to him — and purred even louder. He was actually looking forward to going back to his new home, to being warm, and to lots of good food. And at least he had his own territory there.

All right, so the backyard's a bit small, he thought. *But it'll take me less time to defend it — give me more time to spend sleeping.*

And as soon as I'm in shape again, he decided, *I'm going to find that black tomcat and show him who's boss around here.*

Jenni gave him a big cuddle. "You're all I wanted for Christmas. This is the best Christmas ever." She gave him another kiss. "Merry Christmas, Puss in Boots."